AN INTERACTIVE ADVENTURE SERIES

YOU CHOOSE

THE SPANISH PLOT

LEAH SOKOL

ILLUSTRATED BY
MICHAEL BINIASHVILI

The Spanish Plot

ISBN: 978-1-60763-293-1

Illustrator: Michael Biniashvili
Editor: M. Jakubowicz
Proofreader: Hadassa Goldsmith
Design and layout: Nachum Shapiro

The Judaica Press, Inc.
123 Ditmas Avenue / Brooklyn, NY 11218
718-972-6200 / 800-972-6201
info@judaicapress.com
www.judaicapress.com

Printed in Canada

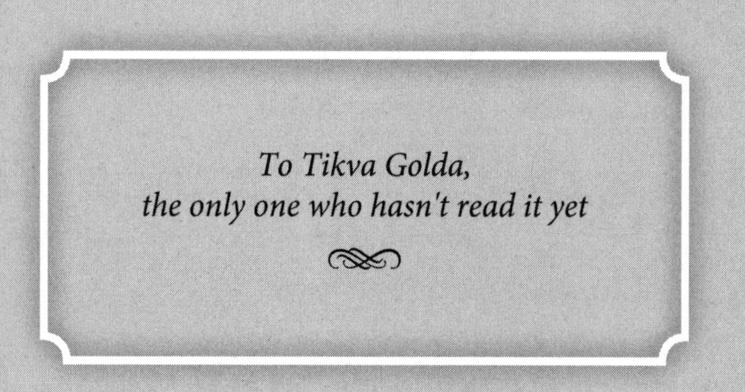

To Tikva Golda,
the only one who hasn't read it yet

YOU ARE WALKING UP the cobblestone street, keeping a close eye on Yitzchak, when you see the man for the first time.

He is not looking at you. He is leaning against a pillar and watching Yitzchak.

Yitzchak is running down the street ahead of you. Every few steps, he falls over. He is only a year and a half old, and advanced for his age, but he is still not that good at running. His little stockings are completely grass-stained, and you know your mother won't be happy — she's going to have to wash them. But he is giggling so much that you haven't made him stop.

The man pushes himself away from the pillar and starts toward you. You're on a narrow street in the Jewish Quarter, and right now, it's empty except for the three of you and a couple of chickens.

You are not easily frightened. But it's the year 1492, and the city of Toledo is not as safe as it used to be. Not for a Jewish child like you.

King Ferdinand and Queen Isabella are thinking of expelling all the Jews from their kingdoms. King Ferdinand rules the kingdom of Aragon, and Queen Isabella rules the kingdom of Castile. Now that they have conquered the kingdom of Granada from the Muslims, they control the entire Spanish Peninsula. They have the power to do whatever they want.

Everyone knows they won't really expel the Jews. Their court is *full* of Jews. Some people even call Queen Isabella "protector of the Jews." (They don't usually mean it as a compliment!)

These rumors are obviously just a way to get the Jews to pay a large bribe. But for some people, it's also an excuse to attack any Jew they see.

This man doesn't look angry or threatening, though. He smiles at you, and his blue eyes are friendly. He is wearing a fur-trimmed velvet cloak, and his fingers glitter with jeweled rings.

What does he want with a common child like you?

You turn your gaze to the spires of the Alcazar, the city's castle. Its towers rise against the swirling clouds.

Maybe this man has come from the court, where Don Yitzchak Abarbanel — little Yitzchak's grandfather — serves the king and queen. Maybe Don Abarbanel has sent him to give you a message.

Your mother works for the Abarbanel family as Yitzchak's nurse. The Abarbanels are rich businessmen, and Don Abarbanel is the financial advisor to the queen. He is also a rabbi and a scholar, and a very kind man. Whenever he comes to see his grandson, you become so shy you forget how to talk. You certainly wouldn't want to embarrass yourself by running away from his messenger.

"Stay where you are, and keep the child with you!" the man calls. There is something in his voice that is not friendly at all.

To wait and hear him out, turn to page 8.

To grab Yitzchak and run, turn to page 11.

To call for help, turn to page 13.

8

As the man comes closer, Yitzchak falls down yet again, and this time he starts to cry. You pick him up, kissing the top of his head to calm him down.

"It's all right," you whisper. "Soon we will be home, and I'll give you an almond cake."

Yitzchak sniffles, but then he smiles. He loves almond cake more than anything. You put him down.

"You must come with me," the man says, stopping several feet away from you. He is breathing heavily. "There is a doctor from Salamanca staying at the castle. Don Abarbanel has convinced him to see his grandson. But you need to bring Yitzchak right away."

As if he understands, Yitzchak coughs.

He has been coughing for a while now, and waking at night.

You know this all too well, because you and your mother share a room with him. It has been weeks since you had a good night's sleep!

So you know Yitzchak hasn't been feeling well. But nobody told you it was serious!

Your mother *has* been very worried lately. You remember an incident from three nights ago. You woke to see your mother holding Yitzchak, and there were tears trickling down her cheeks.

"What's the matter, Mamá?" you asked sleepily.

"Nothing," your mother said. "Nothing. Just politics as usual, up in the castle. You know how it is when the king and queen are in residence."

King Ferdinand and Queen Isabella are always traveling, moving their court from one castle to another. Right now, they live here, in Toledo. It's good news for the merchants, because people from the court like to buy things! But it can also make the town squares too crowded for games.

"Don Abarbanel will take care of it, I am sure," your mother went on. "Go back to sleep."

So you did.

But what if your mother wasn't really worried about what was happening at the castle? What if she was worried about Yitzchak?

"Come quickly," the man snaps. He strokes his short, trimmed beard. "The doctor is a very important man. He does not make a habit of treating Jewish children. He certainly will not wait for you."

"I need to get my mother," you say. "I'm just watching Yitzchak while she takes care of some mending."

"That will take too long. You must come with me right now!"

To run, turn to page 11.

To go with him, turn to page 21.

To insist that you need to ask your mother, turn to page 31.

YOU GRAB YITZCHAK AND bolt. Your hemp sandals slap loudly against the cobblestones as you race past gray stone walls.

Yitzchak is not happy about being grabbed. He squirms in your grasp and claws at your face. You clutch him tighter and keep running.

"Stop it!" the man shouts. You hear the thud-thud of his shoes as he closes the distance between you. "What are you doing, you stupid child? I need to take the boy to the castle to see a doctor! *Stop!*"

You don't stop.

Yitzchak is sobbing hysterically now, and he starts hitting you with his tiny fists. Still, you don't stop.

Not until your foot hits a stone, and you fall.

You twist your body as the ground rushes toward you. Your backbone hits the cobblestones hard, and pain shoots up your spine. But you keep your grip on Yitzchak, so he falls on top of you instead of on the stones.

He screams anyway and shoots out of your arms. By the time you get to your feet, Yitzchak is scrambling away from you as fast as his short legs can carry him — back in the direction you came from.

In order to get Yitzchak, you will have to run straight toward the man — who is still racing at you, shouting furiously. Unless you run in the opposite direction, *right now,* there is no way you can possibly get away from him.

To go after Yitzchak, turn to page 33.

To keep running, turn to page 34.

"HELP!" YOU SCREAM. "SOMEBODY, help me!"

Your screams echo in the empty street. The chickens squawk and scatter. But there is no one close enough to hear you, and the man looks furious.

You scream even louder. "Help me! Please! Somebody!" Then you have an idea. "FIRE!"

Your mother once told you that if you ever need help, you should scream "Fire!" People always come running for a fire, because a fire can spread and hurt everyone.

The man gives you an evil look, then turns and walks away before people can start showing up. Within seconds, he has disappeared from sight.

You pick up Yitzchak and run. Soon you are in a more populated area; you pass mules laden with goods, and several women heading to market. You don't put Yitzchak down until you are right outside Don Abarbanel's home.

But then, of course, Yitzchak clings to you. So you pick him up again, even though your arms hurt, and trudge up the stairs to your mother's room.

Your mother looks up from her mending and tsk-tsks when she sees Yitzchak. "What happened? Did he fall down? Come, Yitzchak, come here."

You hand Yitzchak over and collapse gratefully into a wooden chair.

"It wasn't my fault," you say. "We met a man who frightened me."

"Why? What did he do?"

"Nothing." Now you're embarrassed. "It was silly of me to be scared."

"It's always safer to avoid strange men," your mother says, stroking Yitzchak's dark hair. He puts his head on her shoulder and sniffles, but he is calming down. "Even if it *was* nothing, you made the right choice."

And you can tell she's already stopped thinking about it.

An hour later, when you take Yitzchak to the city's main square, you keep a sharp eye out. But you see no one except the usual buyers and sellers, and a group of men greasing a pole in preparation for the *cucana* — a game to see who can climb the highest up the slippery pole. You hope they start playing soon — Yitzchak loves to watch them slide comically down the pole.

It makes you laugh, too.

Because it's Friday, and your mother is busy preparing for Shabbat, you are in charge of Yitzchak all day. You take him to the mule seller's stall, where he can watch the animals. As he stares in fascination, you open your lunch basket and sneak out some sugared almonds, which you pop into your mouth as you keep an eye on Yitzchak. The glazed nuts crunch between your teeth.

"Ah! I thought I would find you here."

The shout from behind makes you jump. Almonds scatter all over the ground. But a moment later, you recognize the voice.

"You frightened me!" you say. But even though your heart is still pounding, you smile.

Your friend Shimon Seneor grins back at you. He is wearing fur-trimmed clothes and a cloak woven with gold thread, so elegant they almost make you ashamed of your drab woolen clothes.

But even though Shimon's family is rich and important, he has never acted like he is above you. Now, he sits on the grass next to you and waves at Yitzchak. Yitzchak is too busy making faces at the mules to notice.

"What's the news from the castle?" you ask. Shimon's grandfather, like Don Abarbanel, is an advisor at court.

"Not good," Shimon says. He loops his arms around his knees and shakes his head. "My grandfather and your master have offered the king a bribe of 300,000 gold ducats to stop him from expelling the Jews. And they're not even sure that will be enough."

It's a good thing the almonds are scattered on the ground; if you were still eating one, you would choke on it. Don Abarbanel has raised huge sums in the past, to ransom Jewish captives, but *300,000* gold ducats? How can he possibly raise such a fortune? And surely King Ferdinand can't expect the Jews to give *more*?

"Don't worry." Shimon reaches into your basket and takes a sugared almond. "It won't happen. It can't! Jews have been living in this country since before the first Christian ever set foot here. The very name *Toledo* comes from the Hebrew word *tiltul* — wandering. They can't expel us from a city we named!"

"I'm sure you're right," you say. "But —"

You are cut off by a wail from Yitzchak.

Turn to page 17.

YOU JUMP TO YOUR feet and race over. Yitzchak is lying on the ground, his eyes wide and his mouth open in outrage.

"What happened?" you gasp.

"I fell!" Yitzchak says, with enormous indignation.

You kiss the top of his head, then take him with you to sit next to Shimon. Yitzchak immediately gets busy looking through your lunch basket.

"Why are you so jumpy?" Shimon asks, still munching his almonds.

You tell him about the man you saw. Shimon's eyes grow wide.

"Was the man short, with a trimmed beard and thick eyebrows?" he says. "And blue eyes?"

"Yes!" You sit up straight. "You know him?"

"I've seen him at court," Shimon says. "He's a respectable nobleman. I'm sure he wasn't doing anything wrong." He swallows and wipes his mouth with the back of his hand. "Do you want me to ask my grandfather?"

"Yes," you say. "Can we ask him now?"

Shimon nods. "He is probably at the synagogue, learning. Let's go find him."

Your synagogue is the most beautiful building you know of. It was built back when Toledo was under Muslim rule, and it's decorated with graceful arches and delicate carved designs of flowers and leaves. Light shines in through the many narrow windows, illuminating the Hebrew verses inscribed on the holy ark.

There are a few men in the synagogue, learning Torah. Two of them, you know, are Jews who long ago converted to Christianity to save their lives, but they still sneak into the synagogue whenever they can manage it. You and Shimon head over to a second group of men, some of whom you recognize. You've seen them attending Don Abarbanel's *shiurim*—his lessons."

When Shimon asks them where his grandfather is, the oldest man there shakes his head.

"He went back to the castle," he says, "to plead with the king some more."

"We must pray to Hashem," another man sighs. "We must beg Him to change the king's heart."

"Thank you," Shimon says, and draws you away.

"Well," you say, "I guess that's that." You start after Yitzchak, who is running in circles around one of the white marble pillars.

עץ חיים היא

"Not at all!" Shimon says. "Let's go to the castle. If the man had a reason for approaching you, we need to find him."

"What sort of reason?" you say.

"I heard my grandfather say the court was expecting a visit from a famous doctor. Maybe the doctor agreed to look at Yitzchak."

For the past few weeks, Yitzchak has been coughing at night. What if Don Abarbanel asked this doctor to check on him — and *you* took him away?

"If the doctor is here, he's probably not staying long," Shimon says. "We should go to the castle right away. If we're quick enough, we might catch him."

To go with Shimon to the castle, turn to page 60.

To forget the whole thing and take Yitzchak back to the square, turn to page 62.

To go home and ask Don Abarbanel about the man, turn to page 65.

WITH THE MAN AT your side, you walk uphill until you reach the castle.

The closer you get, the more uneasy you become. And once inside the castle, you feel completely out of place. Everything around you is grand and rich. The castle entranceway is a long hallway, with colorful paintings hanging on the stone walls. Through an arched doorway, you enter a large room with an oak table. On it, several noblemen are playing chess. The man leads you past them, onto a staircase leading upward.

You hold Yitzchak's hand tightly, until he gets tired of that and pulls away. Before you can stop him, he trips and falls. He tumbles down a few of the stairs and starts to wail.

The man mutters under his breath. You run quickly and grab Yitzchak.

As you do, you hear a familiar voice from up ahead.

"You need the Jews, Your Majesty! Without them, the economy of the country will come to a halt. And if you require immediate money, we can make you a gift."

"*Abuelo* (Grandfather)!" Yitzchak squeals, and the man claps a hand over his mouth.

"Keep him silent!" he hisses. "Don Abarbanel is speaking to the queen. We must not interrupt them."

You look at him. "But the doctor —"

"The doctor is in his own room. I will take you straight there."

He grabs your arm and drags you farther up the stairs, still keeping one hand over Yitzchak's mouth. You hear Don Abarbanel say, "How much money, Your Majesty, will it take to change your mind?" Then the sound of his voice fades into the distance.

Suddenly, the man yelps and jumps away, waving his hand in the air. There are two small teeth marks in his palm.

"Bad boy!" you say. But your tone makes it sound like "*good boy*," and Yitzchak grins.

"Little brat," the man mutters.

Nobleman or not, you have had enough. You stick your chin up. "Where, exactly, is the doctor?"

The man glares back and lifts his hand to strike you. Just then, a white-haired man wearing a black velvet cloak races around the corner and almost barrels into you.

The blue-eyed man jumps back, drops his hand, and transfers his glare to the newcomer. The white-haired man has a thin nose and a flushed face. Despite his hair, he doesn't look very old.

"Pardon," he says, and brushes past you. You step closer to the wall to let him pass.

"Is that the doctor?" you ask.

"Him?" The blue-eyed man snorts. "No. That's the madman Christopher Columbus, come to beg the queen for ships. He thinks the world is small enough that he can sail right around it." He gestures impatiently. "Come along."

As he turns, a woman walks past you on the stairs, carrying a bundle of linen in her arms. She is between you and the man — this is your chance! Should you grab Yitzchak and run? Or should you continue following the man and see where he intends to take you?

To go with the blue-eyed man, turn to page 25.

To run with Yitzchak, turn to page 30.

"THIS WAY." THE BLUE-EYED man leads you farther into the castle. He pulls you around a corner, into a small, elegant room.

A noblewoman is sitting in the room, head bent over a piece of needlework. She blinks at you, then at Yitzchak, and rises hurriedly to her feet. "Is that —"

"The child we discussed. Yes." Before you can protest, he yanks Yitzchak away from you. "Take him to Johanna's nurse and have her give him some marzipan."

Yitzchak squeals with delight and turns willingly toward her.

"No!" you say. But the woman is fast. She pulls Yitzchak from the room, and the blue-eyed man slams the door behind her with a loud thud.

Fear makes your legs weak. You know, all at once, that you

have made a very big mistake. If only you could go back in time, and choose another path ...

But all you can do is move away. The man follows you, his movements slow and unhurried, until your back is pressed against a tapestry and there is nowhere left to go.

You close your eyes and pray, "*Shema Yisrael* ..."

Then you hear another thud as the door flies open.

Your eyes fly open, too. A Jewish man is standing in the doorway. His craggy face and long, rectangular beard look familiar. Have you seen him before? Yes, you have! A few months ago, when that group of sailors and cartographers came to talk to Don Abarbanel!

"Don Zacuto!" the blue-eyed man says. He steps back from you. "What are you doing here?"

"I am looking for Don Seneor," Don Zacuto says. "Can you take me to him?"

Don Seneor is a friend of Don Abarbanel's. He is also close to the rulers, and uses his position to help the Jews. His grandson, Shimon, is your friend; everything you know about the court, you've heard from Shimon.

"I don't know where Don Seneor is," the blue-eyed man snaps. "Please leave while I attend to some business." He turns back toward you. Don Zacuto shrugs and turns to the door.

"Do you need to send Don Abarbanel a message?" you blurt.

Don Zacuto turns back, his brow wrinkling. "What?"

"I have seen you before!" You speak as quickly as you can. "I am a member of Don Abarbanel's household. And I am a friend of

Shimon Seneor, Don Seneor's grandson." Don Zacuto frowns and your voice trembles, but you keep talking. "Do you want me to send either of them a message? I can deliver it right away."

"Indeed." Don Zacuto looks from you to the blue-eyed man. His eyes narrow, but his voice remains calm. "An excellent idea. Please tell Don Abarbanel that I have made some corrections to my astronomical tables, and I believe that he and Don Seneor would be interested in taking another look at them."

The blue-eyed man presses his lips together, but there is nothing he can do to stop you. You walk right past him, through the door, into the long hallway, and down the stairs.

You are about to break into a run when you hear a child shouting. The sound is coming from below.

You run to a nearby balcony and look out. There, in the inner courtyard of the castle, two children are chasing a yapping dog — and one of the children is Yitzchak!

The children are being watched by a plump woman — a commoner, not the same woman who took Yitzchak a few minutes ago. And Yitzchak, *baruch Hashem*—thank G-d—looks happy. He is giggling as the dog jumps up and tries to lick him.

Your heart is pounding, and you want nothing more than to get out of this castle as fast as possible. But now, you know for *sure* that something is wrong. How can you leave Yitzchak here?

Turn to page 28.

You dash down the stairs and through an archway into the courtyard. When you get close enough for the children to see you, you slow down and take a deep breath.

Yitzchak doesn't notice you. He is too busy wrestling with the dog. But the woman watching him looks up and frowns.

"What are you doing?" she says. "Did they send you from the kitchen?"

"Er ...," you say.

"I asked for salted eels, and they send a simpleton with empty hands?" She snorts. "Go back and tell them the duchess's daughter is hungry. She cannot wait."

"Um," you say.

The woman folds her arms over her chest.

"I'm sorry," you say. "The — uh — the salted eels are not ready.

The cook says it will be just a few more minutes."

"Want *now*!" the little girl says, and folds her own arms in imitation of her nurse. She is wearing a dress with gold thread woven into it, and a black velvet cap set with pearls. Her clothes probably cost more than everything you and your mother own put together.

"Want now, too!" Yitzchak chimes in. Even though he has, of course, never tasted salted eels in his life.

"*Madonna santa* (Good heavens)! Just take both of them to the kitchen, will you?" The woman starts gathering up the toys scattered on the grass. "I'll be along in a minute."

To play along and take both children, turn to page 99.

To say you're just there for Yitzchak, turn to page 101.

YOUR HEART THUDS AGAINST your ribs as you run with all your might, holding Yitzchak tightly against your chest. Your feet hit the ground in fast, uncontrolled thuds. It feels more like you are falling and using your feet to catch yourself than like you are running.

When you get to the bottom of the hill, you risk a glance back. No one is following you.

Your arms and legs hurt, but you don't stop running until you're in the Jewish Quarter. And even then, you walk as quickly as you can, and you don't put Yitzchak down.

Your heart does not stop pounding until you're inside Don Abarbanel's home.

Turn to page 142.

"I AM SORRY," YOU SAY, "but I am not in charge of this child. I am only watching him for my mother. I cannot take him to the castle without her."

You turn and walk away.

Within seconds, the man has caught up to you and grabbed your arm. You try to shake him off, but he is much stronger than you are.

Yitzchak, frightened, struggles to get out of your grasp.

"You're coming with me," the man says. "This is too important to be delayed because of a stupid child."

"Let go of me!" You draw in breath to scream, and he lets go of your arm and claps his hand over your mouth.

You bite down hard. He yelps and lets go, and you dash away, right between his hands. He grabs for you, but you are already too far for him to reach.

Your feet pound the ground as you run, holding Yitzchak tight. You're getting away!

But Yitzchak has had enough. With one final twist, he slides between your arms and hits the cobblestones. With a triumphant shout, he sprints away from you — straight toward the blue-eyed man.

To turn and go after Yitzchak, turn to page 33.

To keep running, turn to page 34.

YOU STUMBLE A FEW steps, then turn and race back. You grab Yitzchak a moment before he reaches the blue-eyed man.

Then the man's hand closes around your arm.

"Stupid child!" he says. "Don Abarbanel wishes for his grandson to see the doctor visiting the castle! What are you doing?"

"I'm sorry," you whisper, trying not to cry. He is holding you so tightly it hurts. "You frightened me, that's all."

"Well, don't be so easily frightened. Come with me."

He doesn't say it like it's a question. He also doesn't let go of your arm.

You have no choice but to do what he says.

Turn to page 21.

YITZCHAK SCREAMS IN OUTRAGE, and you know the man has grabbed him. Guilt pierces you as you round a corner and half-slide down a steep, hilly street.

But you don't turn back.

You dodge around a stray cat, almost trip over a pig, and race past the public oven. You hear the shout of "*Acqu va!*—Water coming!" from above, and know it means someone is about to dump out a chamber pot. Instead of heeding the warning, you keep going, and narrowly miss having the contents of the chamber pot land on your head. You don't even slow down.

When you finally stumble into Don Abarbanel's home, you are sobbing so hard you almost trip over the carpet. The entrance hall is empty but warm, the coals in the large metal brazier giving off flickering heat.

You head toward the stairway, past paintings and tapestries. But someone grabs your arm.

"You're crying!" says a familiar voice. "What's wrong?"

You blink away tears. The face looking at you, dark eyebrows slanted in concern, is familiar. It is Shimon Seneor. He is the grandson of Don Avraham Seneor, who works closely with Don Abarbanel at court. Together, they do their best to gain the friendship of the rulers and protect the Jews.

"What's the matter?" Shimon says. "Did something happen?"

Shimon is being trained to take his grandfather's place at court. You are the child of a servant. Even so, you and Shimon have been friends forever. You want to tell him what happened.

But Shimon is only a year older than you. There is nothing he can do to help, except to sympathize. And as much as you would like sympathy, you know there is no time to waste. You need to find Don Abarbanel and tell him ...

... that you let his grandson get kidnapped.

You imagine the disappointment in Don Abarbanel's deep, kind eyes. A new wave of sobs fills you.

"Don't cry," Shimon says. "Tell me what's wrong. Maybe I can help."

Maybe he can! He can tell his grandfather, and his *grandfather* will tell Don Abarbanel, so you won't have to do it.

Don Seneor will know how to break the news gently. He will immediately come up with a plan to get Yitzchak back. It would be better for everyone if he was the one to tell Don Abarbanel.

To talk to Shimon, turn to page 37.

To insist on seeing Don Abarbanel, turn to page 95.

YOU CANNOT CONTROL YOUR tears as you tell Shimon what happened.

When you are done, Shimon's face is white. He avoids your eyes as he pulls the sleeves of his doublet to straighten them.

"You had better go straight to Don Abarbanel," he says. "I heard he is headed back to the castle, to try to talk the king and queen out of expelling the Jews. Maybe you can catch him before he leaves."

"But can't you ..."

Shimon looks at you, and your voice trails off. You wish you could disappear.

No — you wish you hadn't abandoned Yitzchak. Whatever might have happened to you, it can't be worse than the shame you feel now.

"You're right," you say, in a low voice. "I'll go."

"Or," Shimon says slowly, "we could go to the castle instead."

"What?"

"I've been to the castle with my grandfather many times." Shimon's voice rises in excitement. "Maybe I can help you find Yitzchak."

He starts toward the door, then glances back to see if you're following.

To go to Don Abarbanel, turn to page 95.

To follow Shimon to the castle, turn to page 39.

THE WAY TO THE castle is straight uphill. By the time you get there, your legs ache and your muscles burn. But as Shimon leads you through the castle courtyard, you get a chance to catch your breath.

The courtyard is full of people — noblemen in velvet hats, noblewomen in huge hoop skirts, and traveling salesmen shouting out prices. Servant boys — some no older than you — run around holding rolled-up papers and trying to look important.

Shimon leads you confidently through the castle entranceway. You walk into a long hallway, with colorful paintings hanging on the stone walls. Then you pass under an arched doorway and enter a grand room with an oak table. Around it, several noblemen sit playing chess. You glance over and see that they are playing the new version of the game, in which the queen is the most

powerful piece — a rule people have adopted out of respect for Queen Isabella's power.

Shimon leads you past them, toward a staircase leading upward. You know you don't belong here. Everything is too grand and rich, too overwhelming and intimidating. But Shimon seems to know where he is going. He strides up the stairs, and you rush to follow.

"Hurry up!" Shimon says. "We must find my grandfather."

Turn to page 42.

You follow Shimon up the stairs.

The upper floor of the castle is all rectangular stone and arched halls, with huge tapestries hung over the walls. You are walking past a half-open door when you hear someone say, "Your Majesty, you will be no different from the others who have tried to destroy us."

You recognize the voice. It's Don Abarbanel! He's already at the castle.

You peek around the edge of the door.

Don Abarbanel is standing before Queen Isabella, who sits on a velvet-backed chair. She is wearing a gown that shimmers with jewels, and her reddish hair is held back by a headdress covered with pearls. She is beautiful, but her face is cold.

"The Jews have outlived all the nations that waged war against

us," Don Abarbanel continues. "And G-d will punish those who try to destroy His nation."

"Enough!" the queen says.

Her tone is so frightening that you jump and dislodge a small painting from the wall. It plummets to the floor. You catch it a moment before it hits.

The queen's eyes flicker toward the door. You hold your breath, too scared to move. Shimon's face has gone white.

The queen looks back at Don Abarbanel.

"It is not I who put this expulsion idea into the king's heart," she says. "Even if you convinced me, I could not change his mind." She draws herself up. "But you have not convinced me."

Don Abarbanel closes his eyes. He looks, for a moment, very old.

"But *you*," the queen says, "are a wise man, Don Abarbanel. You have advised me well for many years. I do not wish to lose your services."

"Then you must let the Jews remain in your lands," Don Abarbanel says. "For I will go where my people go."

"Be reasonable," the queen says. "Convert. Be baptized. You will keep your house and your wealth. Your family will stay together. You will remain in our service, and you can do much to help those members of your people who have made the same choice."

There is a moment of silence. You close your eyes. Suddenly — too late — you understand.

"*Your family will stay together ....*"

Now you know why Yitzchak was kidnapped.

"Never," Don Abarbanel says. His voice is no longer loud and thunderous, but it is very clear. "I am a Jew. I love this country, but if I have to leave, I will. I will run to the farthest corners of the earth before I will ever abandon my faith."

The queen hisses in fury, "Then do so. You may leave our presence at once."

"Your Majesty." Don Abarbanel draws himself up. "The Jews will outlive you and your nation. You will be remembered forever, not for your accomplishments or your conquests, but for *this*."

The queen stares at him, and suddenly, you remember to be terrified. You slide slowly backward along the wall. Shimon tiptoes toward you. Together, you creep down the hall until you have turned several corners and are safely out of earshot.

"What are you thinking?" Shimon says. "You look like someone punched you!"

"I know the rulers' plan," you gasp. "They want to baptize Yitzchak, in order to force his parents — and his grandfather — to convert to Christianity."

"No!" Shimon says. "That cannot be."

"It's true." You clench your fists, and then suddenly realize something. "But the queen did not mention Yitzchak! She told Don Abarbanel he should convert, but she didn't tell him that he *had* to convert in order to keep his grandson."

"Maybe she's waiting for a better time," Shimon says.

"Or maybe," you say, "Yitzchak hasn't been baptized yet. Maybe we can still stop it."

"How?"

"I don't know. We have to tell Don Abarbanel that Yitzchak is here."

"No!" Shimon says. "We can't interrupt his audience with the queen. And there is nothing he can do, anyhow."

Shimon may be right. But ... if *anyone* can do something, surely it is Don Abarbanel.

"We should tell *my* grandfather," Shimon says.

That's a good idea. Shimon's grandfather is even closer to the king and queen than Don Abarbanel. They say that years ago, he even helped arrange King Ferdinand and Queen Isabella's marriage, and helped them keep it a secret from Queen Isabella's brother. If Queen Isabella trusted Don Seneor then, surely she will listen to him now!

"Come with me," Shimon urges. "My grandfather will be able to help us."

To go with Shimon, turn to page 47.

To wait for Don Abarbanel, turn to page 49.

SHIMON LEADS YOU THROUGH the hallways and up more stairs. Even here, deep in the castle, the walls are covered with splendid tapestries and the floors are layered with heavy carpets.

But you have no time to gape. Your mind is too full of what you know, and of the terrible situation Don Abarbanel is in. The terrible situation you are all in.

Finally, you reach a room with a slightly open door. Through it, you hear the familiar voice of Shimon's grandfather.

You step into the room. Shimon closes the door.

Shimon's grandfather, Don Seneor, glances at you before focusing on Shimon. "I'm glad you're here. There is something I must tell you." He looks back at you. "And you should hear it, too."

"What is going on?" you say.

"Sit down." Don Seneor gestures to a carved wooden chair.

Reluctantly, you sit. Don Seneor clasps his hands behind his back.

"Don Abarbanel and I have failed," he says sadly. "Despite all our entreaties, and all our bribes, we cannot change the king's mind. He is going to expel all the Jews from Spain."

"But Don Abarbanel is speaking to the queen," you say. "We heard him. She was still listening . . . ."

"Perhaps. But even if Don Abarbanel succeeds, her priest, Friar Torquemada, will sway her back. There is no hope." Don Seneor begins to pace across the room. His satin shoes make almost no sound on the thick carpet. "We will have three months to leave. And we will not be allowed to take anything we own with us."

You can hardly believe what he is saying. But his voice is serious, and oddly calm. "There are few places where we can go. Most Jews, probably, will cross the border to Portugal. But Don Abarbanel cannot even do that. He has too many enemies in the Portuguese court, and already once barely escaped Portugal with his life."

Why is he telling you this?

"A journey by ship will cost a fortune. And pirates will be waiting, as soon as they understand what is happening here." Don Seneor turns to face you. "But there is one other option."

You stare at him, waiting for him to go on.

Turn to page 51.

"I'M WAITING HERE," YOU say. "When Don Abarbanel comes out from his audience with the queen, I'll tell him what I know."

"You can't do that!" Shimon hisses. "It's dangerous. We have no business here. And if whoever is *behind* the plan finds out that you know —"

He breaks off suddenly, looking over your shoulder.

You turn.

An old man is striding in your direction. He is wearing a long white robe covered by a large black cloak. His entire head is shaved, except for a ring of hair that encircles his bald scalp. His face is set in a scowl.

A servant scurries up beside him. "Friar Torquemada! The queen is in an audience —"

"I know she is," the friar growls. He does not stop walking.

Torquemada! You gasp and draw back.

Every Jew knows the name of Friar Torquemada. He is the official in charge of the Spanish Inquisition, and his goal in life is to make sure that Jews who converted to Christianity are not secretly practicing Judaism. He is very close to the queen and has great influence over her. They say he is doing his best to convince her to expel the Jews. He thinks the faithful Jews are bad influences on the Jews who have converted to Christianity.

And now, he is about to interrupt Don Abarbanel's audience and ruin Don Abarbanel's one chance to convince the queen to change her mind.

You hesitate. Is there some way you can stop him? But *that* would be more dangerous than anything you've done so far. And it probably wouldn't work. The smart thing would be to get out of his way.

"Come *on*!" Shimon whispers. His voice is shaking.

To follow Shimon, turn to page 54.

To try and stop Torquemada, turn to page 57.

"Convert to Christianity," Shimon fills in, without meeting your eyes. His voice rises shrilly. "If we convert to Christianity, we can stay, and we can keep everything we own. Our lives can go on exactly as before."

This is not a new idea. There are many, many Christians in Spain who used to be faithful Jews, until they were attacked by mobs and chose conversion instead of death. Some of them still remain as close to the Jewish community as they can, and practice Judaism in secret. Others have attached themselves to their new religion — and some of those have become the worst enemies of the Jews, as if they are trying to prove how not-Jewish they now are.

So maybe you shouldn't be as shocked as you are. But it takes you several minutes to even find your voice, and then all you can manage is a splutter.

"It is an impossible choice," Don Seneor says sadly. "But one that every single Jew in Spain is going to have to make. And we have made ours."

You stare at him, then whirl around to stare at Shimon. This time, he does meet your gaze.

"I'm sorry," Shimon says. "But my family has already discussed this. We are staying here. As Christians."

You are too shocked to say anything.

"We have no choice," Shimon says, in a pleading voice. "Our family has lived here for generations. This is our home. We can't leave."

Your family has been Jewish for longer than you have been Spanish, you think. But you don't say it, because you understand Shimon. Who could possibly bear to leave Spain behind forever?

"You can stay, too," Shimon adds.

"No!" you say.

"Your conversion doesn't have to be real. Secretly, in your heart — and when you're alone in your home — you can still be a Jew."

That's not really being a Jew, is it? you think. But you say nothing.

"If you leave," Shimon says, "where will you go? Who will take you in?"

You don't know the answer to that, and Shimon sees it in your face. He leans forward.

"Just think about it," he says. "Promise me you'll consider it."

Your fists clench. You want to tell him no. That you will always be a faithful Jew, no matter what. That you cannot believe he is willing to throw his faith aside so easily.

But if you do, he will say no more. You will never find out what else he knows.

Besides — he is your friend. You don't want to lose him. You don't want to lose everything you have and everything you know.

To say no, turn to page 121.

To say you'll think about it, turn to page 139.

As you turn the corner, Torquemada flings the door open. Don Abarbanel is abruptly silent. The queen lets out an outraged gasp.

The friar's voice is so loud you can hear it clearly. "What does this Jew offer you," he says, "to abandon your duty to your god?"

There is a crash as he throws something down.

Don Abarbanel speaks up, his voice muffled. But Torquemada interrupts him.

"Spain can never be united until all its people share the same, true faith," he says in a ringing voice. "God will not bless us while we tolerate heretics."

The queen draws in a breath, then lets out a small sob. And you know that whatever chance Don Abarbanel had to convince her — it is now gone.

But there is nothing you can do. You duck your head and hurry after Shimon.

You turn a corner and find yourself at a window that looks into the inner courtyard. There are two children in the courtyard, a boy and a girl, playing with balls.

You stop short and stare. The boy is Yitzchak! And no one is watching him.

"Yitzchak!" you shout, before you can think better of it.

Both children look up. The girl wrinkles her nose. Yitzchak's face lights up, and he drops his ball to the ground.

"Wait there!" you say, but he is already running toward the stairs.

The girl watches him go, her brow furrowed. You hold your breath, afraid she is going to shout for help.

Instead, she walks over to the ball Yitzchak dropped. She picks it up and clutches it to her chest, her lips curving into a smug smile.

Then Yitzchak hurtles around the corner and throws himself at you. You grab him and hold him tight. Not until you see a drop of wetness on his black hair do you realize that you are crying.

"Let's get out of the castle, quick!" you gasp.

Shimon shakes his head. "We can't. We still don't know what's going on or why he's here."

"I'm not leaving him behind," you say firmly.

"Let's take him to my grandfather, then." Shimon turns and keeps going, and you follow. Yitzchak squirms, so you put him down, but you keep a firm grip on his hand.

Turn to page 113.

"FRIAR!" YOU CRY, RACING down the hall. "There is an emergency! You must come!"

Torquemada looks down at you. His lip curls. "Move aside, child."

"It's really important! Please! I beg you." Your mind races. What would convince Torquemada to pause?

You glance back at Shimon, and suddenly you remember a fragment of a conversation you overheard last week, between Don Abarbanel and Shimon's grandfather. They were talking about how to raise money for a bribe, and Don Seneor had insisted that no amount of money would be enough to change Torquemada's mind.

"His real concern," Don Seneor had said, "is the *conversos*, those Jews who have already, tragically, converted to Christianity.

Torquemada doesn't trust them, and he thinks that the faithful Jews are helping them keep the mitzvot in secret."

"It's about a group of *conversos*!" you say quickly. "They are … they are plotting with Jews! Against the king, and against you!"

Torquemada's eyes blaze, and he stops walking. You draw in a huge breath. You've mentioned the one thing he is truly worried about, and it worked!

Or did it? Torquemada is still scowling. "And why, exactly, is this my concern?"

"Um." You swallow hard. "One of the plotters says he'll confess, but only to you."

Torquemada glares at you. "What is his name?"

"I — uh — I don't dare say."

"Where are they?"

"In the — in the courtyard —"

But your answers aren't coming fast enough. Torquemada's eyes narrow in suspicion, and he sweeps you to the side. You stagger against the wall, hitting your arm on the stone.

As you blink back tears of pain, Torquemada strides past you, his black cloak fluttering behind him.

The door to the room swings fully open, and Don Abarbanel walks out with the queen. Both are smiling.

"Your Majesty!" Torquemada says. "I must protest —"

"Not now," Queen Isabella says. "Don Abarbanel and I have come to an agreement." She nods at Don Abarbanel. "Three hundred thousand gold ducats, yes? You are sure you can come up with it?"

You stifle a gasp. That's a fortune! But Don Abarbanel nods. "You will have it within a week, even if I have to provide it entirely on my own."

"No!" Torquemada says. "The Jews are heretics. Do not allow them to bribe you, Your Majesty!"

Queen Isabella's eyebrows slash downward.

"I am your queen," she says, in a low, steely voice. "And my decision is made."

Torquemada snarls in fury.

You slip quickly back the way you came, before he can think to look for the child who delayed him.

Turn to page 147.

THE WAY TO THE castle is straight uphill. By the time you get there, your legs ache and your muscles burn. But as Shimon leads you through the castle courtyard, you get a chance to catch your breath.

The courtyard is full of people—noblemen in velvet hats, noblewomen in huge hoop skirts, and traveling salesmen shouting out prices. Servant boys—some no older than you—run around holding rolled-up papers and trying to look important.

Yitzchak pulls at your arm and points. You follow his gaze. Near the stables, a group of servants is setting up lances for yet another jousting tournament—part of the celebrations over the fall of Granada, the last Muslim stronghold on the Spanish Peninsula. King Ferdinand and Queen Isabella conquered Granada almost three months ago, but it seems the festivities are not over yet.

Shimon leads you confidently through the castle entranceway. You walk into a long hallway, with colorful paintings hanging on the stone walls. Through an arched doorway, you enter a grand room with an oak table. Around it, several noblemen sit playing chess. You glance over and see that they are playing the new version of the game, in which the queen is the most powerful piece — a rule people have adopted out of respect for Queen Isabella's power.

You know you don't belong here. Everything is too grand and rich, too overwhelming and intimidating. But Shimon seems to know where he is going. He strides up the stairs, and you rush to follow.

"No run!" Yitzchak whines. "Legs hurt!"

You know exactly how he feels.

Turn to page 113.

"THERE IS SOMETHING NOT right about this," you say. "I want nothing to do with this doctor."

"Are you sure?"

"Yes, I'm sure," you say. "Let's forget the whole thing." You shrug. "Come to the scribe's house instead. Let's find out what his children are doing today."

For a moment, you think Shimon will say no. Lately, he considers himself too old to have fun. But he surprises you by nodding. "Sure," he says. "Why not?"

You spend the morning playing bocce, your favorite ball game, with Yitzchak running around and messing up the balls every chance he gets. By the time you get home, tired and sweaty, you have almost forgotten the strange man.

Later that evening, as you stand next to your mother and

watch her light the Shabbat candles, you feel tired but peaceful. Your hair is still wet from your bath, and Yitzchak is curled up near the fireplace, almost asleep. Your mother finishes the blessing and hugs you, and you breathe in the smell of orange peels. It is Shabbat now, a time to rest and pray — just as it was last week, just as it will be every week, for the rest of your life. You feel safe.

But when you wake up the next morning, it is to the sound of your mother screaming.

"He's gone! Yitzchak? Yitzchak!"

You rush over to her bed, where Yitzchak usually sleeps.

"He must have gotten out," you say, but your heart sinks in your chest. "He must be hiding. We will find him."

"No, no! He would never do that." Your mother covers her face with her hands. "And there is a smell in the room, of sweat and dirt. Someone has taken him. What will we do? I must tell Don Abarbanel!"

She dresses swiftly and leaves the room. You are terrified — for Yitzchak, and for yourself, too. Your mother is a widow; you are only able to survive because of the Abarbanel family's charity in taking her on as a nursemaid and letting you live here. What will they do if they think it was her fault their child was taken?

What will they do if they realize it was *your* fault? That you knew something was wrong, and you told no one?

They don't have to realize, you think. After all, it is too late for it to make a difference. The only thing you can do now is ruin your mother's life.

But are you sure it won't make a difference?

You're not. And so you know you don't really have a choice.

Turn to page 69.

"I DON'T HAVE ANY BUSINESS going to the castle," you say. "I'm going to take Yitzchak home and tell his grandfather about this."

Shimon shrugs. "If that's what you think is best. I'll see you later."

But Don Abarbanel, of course, is not home. Like Shimon's grandfather, he is in the castle, trying to reason with the king and queen.

You should have thought of that.

You hang around the house, playing bocce with Yitzchak, hoping Don Abarbanel will return soon. But he does not. Instead, a messenger arrives from the castle, with instructions for Don Abarbanel's son.

"Don Abarbanel has told the king he will give him 300,000 gold ducats if he allows the Jews to stay!" a servant whispers to you. "And much of that will come out of his own funds! His son has to start preparing."

You don't get a chance to find out more. Before you know it, your mother calls you, and you are kept busy helping prepare for Shabbat.

Later that evening, as you stand next to your mother and watch her light the Shabbat candles, you cannot shake your feeling of unease. Your mother finishes the *brachah,* or blessing, and hugs you. Your hair is still damp from your bath, and you can smell the orange peels your mother used to scent your bath water. Usually, this is the time of week when you feel safest and happiest.

But Don Abarbanel has still not returned from the castle.

That night, you cannot sleep.

You lie in the room you share with your mother, your stomach full of food, staring up at the ceiling. Images from the day keep running through your mind. The blue-eyed man. Yitzchak clinging to you. The Alcazar, grim and formidable, rising against the sky.

You roll over and bury your head in your pillow. You squeeze your eyes shut and try to will yourself to sleep.

Of course, that never works.

So you try to think of something pleasant. In just a couple of weeks, the king is going to be holding yet another joust, to celebrate the conquest of Granada. You will be able to watch the knights ....

No, that's not working, either. You're less close to sleep than ever.

Thud!

You startle and roll onto your side—just in time to see a dark shape, the outline of a man, climbing in through the window.

How's your self-control?

If you scream, turn to page 70.

If you manage to stay quiet, turn to page 72.

If you manage to stay quiet, then think it over and decide that screaming is actually the smart thing to do in this situation, turn to page 70.

When you reach Don Abarbanel's study, his door is open and his face is ghostly white.

You force yourself to walk into the room. Before you can lose your courage, you gasp, "I know where he might be!"

You manage to get out what has happened. Then you burst into tears.

Through blurry eyes, you watch Don Abarbanel race out of the room.

Turn to page 148.

"AAAUUUGGHHHH!"

Even you didn't know you could scream that loud. But Yitzchak is even louder when he's just been woken up.

"WAAAAHHHHH!"

Both of your screams, together, can probably be heard at the castle. The dark figure freezes.

Your mother sits up in bed and sees the man. Her screams join yours and Yitzchak's. Outside the room, a door slams and footsteps come running.

The man turns back to the window. In the bright moonlight, you can see his face. It is the blue-eyed man who approached you earlier!

Your bed is closest to the window. If you lunge, maybe you can grab his ankles and pull him down.

Or you can get kicked in the face.

And even if you succeed — what then? What if no one else gets here in time? What if he has a knife?

He's leaving. Maybe you should just let him leave.

As you crouch on your bed, he hoists himself up to the window.

It's now or never. What are you going to do?

To grab his ankles, turn to page 73.

To let him go, turn to page 79.

It's so quiet you can hear your own heartbeat, like the sound of distant marching. The man lowers himself into the room.

You don't move a single finger. You wonder how it's possible that *he* can't hear your heartbeat, too.

The man walks quietly toward your mother's bed. He lifts Yitzchak up, carefully extricating Yitzchak's foot from under your mother's elbow. Your mother mutters and rolls over, but does not wake up. Yitzchak's snores get a little louder, but he lies limply over the man's shoulder.

The man starts toward the door.

If you decide to scream now, turn to page 137.

If you follow him, turn to page 81.

YOU LEAP WITH ALL your might and grab the man's ankles.

As expected, he kicks back at you. But you are prepared for that. You jerk your head sideways, and his mud-encrusted boot barely misses your cheek.

Then you both fall backward onto the floor.

You land flat on your back, and the man lands on top of you. He is *heavy*! Pain shoots up your spine as you hit the floor, and your chest feels like it's being crushed. Then, just in case that wasn't enough, the man's elbow hits you right under the eye.

He rolls off you, and you are finally able to breathe. But when he springs back toward the window, you jump to your feet and throw yourself at him again.

This time, *you* land on top of *him*, but somehow his head still manages to smash into your face. You howl, grab his hair, and pull. He turns and flings you off with a sweep of his arm. You fly across the room, crash into the side of a large wooden chest, and slide to the floor.

Then the door bursts open, and the room is full of men.

You close your eyes against the blinding pain in your head. But you cannot close your ears against the noise, and it hammers at your skull: shouts and curses and clangs.

Since closing your eyes isn't helping, you force them open. The blue-eyed man is on the floor, flat on *his* back, with several of the household servants holding him down. Don Abarbanel and his son — Yitzchak's father — stand over him.

"Tell us," Don Abarbanel says. "Why were you sneaking into my home?"

The man spits on the floor, then presses his lips together.

"I will find out," Don Abarbanel says. "It will go easier for you if you just tell me now."

Silence.

"Very well, then," Don Abarbanel says. "Put him in the empty wine cellar, and lock the door. We'll see what he has to say in the morning."

The man sneers. But he gets obediently to his feet.

When it is only the three of you in the room again, your mother comes over to tuck you in. She hugs you tight, and you feel her trembling.

Yitzchak is back asleep within minutes, his soft snores filling the room. But you're pretty sure your mother doesn't fall asleep again.

And you know for certain that you don't.

Turn to page 76.

THE NEXT MORNING, AFTER synagogue, the whole house is abuzz with news about last night's escapade. The story has grown; now people are saying there were two men, and a sword fight, and blood splattered everywhere.

"I heard you disarmed the man yourself!" your friend Shimon exclaims.

You look down modestly and smile.

But even though you listen to every bit of gossip you can catch, one thing is clear: No one knows who the man is, or what he wants with Yitzchak.

You have very little to do today. Normally, you spend most of Shabbat looking after Yitzchak. After last night's scare, though, none of the grownups are willing to let him out of their sight.

As far as you can tell, Yitzchak is enjoying the attention.

So you wander around Don Abarbanel's home, hoping to overhear an important piece of news. You are alone in a hallway when someone hisses at you.

"Child! You! Come here!"

You recognize the voice even before you turn.

The blue-eyed man peers at you through the small window of the wine cellar door. The door is latched shut.

"Come here," he says.

"Um," you say. "I don't think so."

"The baby — Yitzchak. You want him safe, don't you?"

"Yes," you snap. "I do. That's why I'm staying far away from you."

"You think this is about *me*?" His laugh sounds like it's scraping the inside of his throat. "Fool. If I don't come back, they will just send someone else."

"Who's *they*?" you demand.

"That's what the rabbi wants to know. He said he'll let me go if I tell him, but I don't trust Jews." He leans forward, his eyes bright. "You're different, though. You're just a child. You haven't learned how to lie yet. I'll tell *you* the truth, if you promise to let me go."

"Sure," you say. "I believe that."

He shrugs. "All right, then. Walk away. And when someone else comes to grab your precious Yitzchak, you'll have only yourself to blame."

To hear him out, turn to page 86.

To walk away, turn to page 88.

AS THE MAN TUMBLES out through the window, you rush to your mother's bed, shouting.

Within minutes, it seems, the whole house is awake. And by the time you and your mother get dressed, Don Abarbanel is already gone — determined, another servant tells you, to find out why someone was breaking into his home.

It seems like forever before Don Abarbanel returns. When he does, he summons you to his study.

Don Abarbanel's study is a small, elegant room, full of books and the smell of ink. When you enter, Don Abarbanel smiles at you.

"I owe you my gratitude," he says. "That man was coming to kidnap my grandson. Thanks to you, I now know what is going on, and I have taken steps to stop it."

You say something that comes out sounding like, "*Gah — ah — blark.*"

Don Abarbanel's eyes are deep and wise. "There will be difficult times ahead for the Jewish people. The king and queen, despite all my efforts, will not change their minds. Soon, we will all have to leave our homes behind, forever." His shoulders rise and fall. "But as long as we are all together, with Hashem's help, we will make it through. You and your mother will always have a place with my family. I will make sure you are both safe."

This time, you manage actual words. "Thank you."

Don Abarbanel smiles. "And now, I believe, you need to go back to bed."

Turn to page 141.

THE MAN DOES NOT bother to close the door behind him. Which makes it easier for you to creep out of bed and follow him into the hall.

But as you turn the corner, you trip and fall to your knees. The thud shatters the silence.

The man glances back, then turns and races for the door, holding Yitzchak tightly against his shoulder. Before you have a chance to make another move, he is down the stairs and out the front door.

You race after him, but you are too late. The street outside is empty.

Then you hear a familiar cry.

Yitzchak!

You take off in the direction of the cry, running through a maze of tight lanes, past doors set between archways and ceilings. You dash past the public oven and skid around a corner, just in time to see Yitzchak racing down the street, away from you. The kidnapper is getting to his feet. By the light of the full moon, you can see a bite mark on his hand, and fury on his face.

He starts after Yitzchak, making a sound that is almost a snarl.

To attack him, turn to page 83.

To turn and run in the other direction, turn to page 85.

Before the man can take another step, you throw yourself onto his back.

He shouts in surprise and twists, reaching over his shoulders to rip you off. You cling to him with all your might. His hands rake across your head, yanking out clumps of hair, sending pain burning across your scalp. Then he grabs your arm and flings you off him, throwing you hard against a nearby building.

You crash into the stones and slide to the ground. It hurts so much you can't manage to get to your feet. You can't even see. You are completely helpless.

But the street is no longer silent. The sound of the struggle has brought people out of their homes, and they are not happy about being woken up on a Friday night.

Within seconds, their grumbles turn to shouts of alarm and anger.

When you finally drag yourself upright, you see the kidnapper surrounded by a mass of Jewish men, loudly demanding to know what he is doing here.

You force yourself to your feet. Every muscle in your body feels bruised, and your throat is tight. But you manage to raise your voice. "That man was sneaking into Don Abarbanel's house!"

All the men turn to face you. Past them, you can see the kidnapper glaring at you.

"For what purpose?" one of the men demands. You recognize him as Reuben, the armor maker, a tall, stocky man with thick forearms.

"I don't know," you say.

The kidnapper sneers. "And you never will."

"We'll see about that," another man says. "Let's take him to Don Abarbanel."

When you reach Don Abarbanel's house, you find Yitzchak waiting in front of the main door. You grab him and hug him as tightly as you can.

Turn to page 76.

THE MAN IS SO big, and so angry-looking. You back away, the cobblestones slippery under your feet, and then you turn and run.

In Don Abarbanel's home, everyone is still asleep. At least, they are until you start screaming.

You are sobbing so hard you can barely get the story out. But you do, and as soon as you finish, men from the household race out the door.

You are almost calm when they finally return, downcast and empty-handed.

Yitzchak is gone.

Turn to page 150.

"WHY?" YOU SAY. "WHY will someone come grab him? Who is after him?"

"Unlock this door and I'll tell you."

You shake your head.

"All right. Promise that you'll open it *after* I tell you."

"I will," you say.

"Promise it on your ... your holy book. What's it called? Your *Torah*." He pronounces the word strangely, like he can't wait to get it out of his mouth. "Promise on your Torah that once I tell you the truth, you'll open the door."

You hesitate. In Jewish law, breaking a promise is a terrible sin. Among Christians and Muslims, too, no one wants to be known as someone who breaks his word.

But you know you can't let this man out.

"I won't hurt you," he says, as if reading your thoughts. "Once I've betrayed my employer, all I will want is to get out of town. I won't touch you. I'll just leave. That's *my* promise."

You swallow hard.

"Go on," the man says. "You want to save him, don't you? Promise."

To promise, turn to page 90.

To walk away, turn to page 88.

YOU TURN YOUR BACK on the wine cellar and walk down the hall. Shivers of fear go up your legs, but you keep moving.

"Stupid child!" the man shouts. "You've lost your chance to help your master! When he loses everything, it will be your fault!"

You don't turn around. Instead, you go straight to Don Abarbanel's study and you tell him everything.

"You did the right thing," Don Abarbanel says as soon as you are finished. "Never trust a man who tries to make bargains with a child. Walking away was the smartest choice you could have made."

His voice is so kind. Somehow, it is *that* — the softness of his voice — that finally makes tears spill over your eyelashes.

"But now we'll never find out who sent him!" you say.

Don Abarbanel's smile tightens.

"Oh, I think we will," he says. "A man like that cares about only one thing: money. All I have to do is match the price of whoever hired him." He stands. "And you learned one important fact from him: Other men are coming, and Yitzchak is still in danger. Which means that I cannot wait until Shabbat ends to begin bargaining with him."

He strides out the door, leaving you alone to get your tears under control.

Turn to page 97.

YOU CLENCH YOUR FISTS hard. Your palms are hot and sweaty.

"I promise," you say.

"On your holy book!"

"I promise," you say again. "Tell me the truth and I'll let you go." You lean forward. "Who wants Yitzchak?"

"I don't know *exactly* who," the man says.

You throw your arms up. "Then why —"

"But I can tell you the plan." He pauses, waiting for you to ask. You force yourself to remain silent, and finally he says, "I was instructed not to harm the child, not even to hit or scratch him." His voice is so casual it sends a chill up your spine. You want to run upstairs, hug Yitzchak tight, and kiss his smooth cheek.

But it's more important for you to be *here,* finding out the truth. You hope.

The man lowers his voice, forcing you to walk closer so you can hear him. "They want him to look nice for his baptism."

You jerk back.

The man laughs. "*That*'s the plan. Baptize the child and make him a Christian. Once he's Christian, of course, he can't legally be raised by Jews. So if his family wants him back, *they'll* have to be baptized, too. Then the king and queen can expel the Jews and still keep Don Abarbanel as their financial advisor."

You stare at him, unable to speak or move. He leans back and folds his arms over his chest.

"I kept my part of our bargain. Now you keep yours. Let me go."

To open the door, turn to page 92.

To run, turn to page 94.

THE KIDNAPPER'S EYES GLEAM as he watches you approach. Fear makes your legs feel shivery, but you force yourself forward. You have no choice. You *promised.*

You unlatch the door, then step back quickly. The man lunges out of the room. You see his fierce smile, and then, too late, his fist swinging toward you.

And that's the last thing you see for a while.

When you regain consciousness, you are back in your room and your mother is sitting next to your bed. You try to sit up, and a splitting pain whips through your skull, forcing you to lie back down with a groan.

"Don't move," your mother says swiftly. "You had a nasty blow to your head."

You close your eyes — the sunlight hurts them — and whisper, "Yitzchak?"

Your mother's sob tells you all you need to know.

"I know where he was taken," you manage. "And I know why. You must tell Don Abarbanel."

You manage to get the story out, even though talking hurts more with every word. When you're finally done, you fall gratefully into the blackness of sleep, as your mother's footsteps hurry toward the door.

When you wake again, you are alone.

So you can cry as much as you want.

Turn to page 150.

YOU TURN AND WALK away.

"Liar!" the man shouts after you. "Coward! Jewish swine!"

His words ring in your ears.

"Don't you dare tell anyone what I said, do you hear me? Not until you let me go! You made a *promise*!"

You imagine you can hear his shouts all the way to Don Abarbanel's study.

Don Abarbanel is learning Torah, concentrating fiercely, his lips moving slightly as he studies. But when he sees you, he immediately looks up.

"I know," you say, your voice shaking, "why that man came for Yitzchak."

Turn to page 158.

Don Abarbanel's study is a small, elegant room, full of books and the smell of ink. But it is empty, and when you ask a passing servant, he tells you Don Abarbanel is up in the castle.

You go back out to the entrance hall, but Shimon is already gone.

You don't know what to do, so you wait in the study. You think of all the times you have passed by this room and seen Don Abarbanel bent over a scroll, or covering pages and pages with his writing. You remember all the times you've caught Yitzchak trying to sneak in here, and the one time he managed to get past you and spill ink all over Don Abarbanel's desk.

You concentrate on not crying. You mostly succeed.

After what seems like forever, Don Abarbanel walks into the

study, looking weary. But when he sees you, he manages a smile. "Is something wrong?"

You take a deep breath and tell him everything that happened. As you speak, your tears begin to fall, and you don't try to stop them.

"I'm sorry," you finish. By now, you are sobbing so hard you can barely get the words out.

"No, no. You did the right thing in coming to me." He holds his head in his hands. "Who could be behind this? It must be one of my enemies at court ...."

He rushes out the door. "Stay here!" he calls over his shoulder. "Wait for me. I may send someone with more questions."

Turn to page 148.

IT SEEMS LIKE FOREVER before Don Abarbanel returns. You pace the floor, looking at the spines of his many books, their titles in Hebrew and Latin and Portuguese.

Finally, the door opens and Don Abarbanel walks in. His face is grave, but when he sees you, he smiles. Yitzchak toddles in after him, and even though he's not usually allowed in the study, Don Abarbanel says nothing.

"Did you find out what the man was after?" you whisper.

Turn to page 145.

IT SEEMS LIKE FOREVER before Don Abarbanel returns. You pace the floor, looking at the spines of the many books lining his shelves, their titles in Hebrew and Latin and Portuguese.

Finally, the door opens and Don Abarbanel walks in.

Beside him, holding his hand, is Yitzchak.

"You found him!" you gasp, and burst into tears of relief.

Turn to page 145.

"COME ALONG, CHILDREN," YOU say, and hold out your hands.

Yitzchak, of course, takes your hand immediately. The girl sticks her thumb into her mouth and considers you.

She looks like she's going to refuse to come with you. You hope so. That would make things a lot easier.

But then she toddles over to you and puts her wet hand in yours.

You sigh, and the woman looks over her shoulder at you. You walk quickly out of the courtyard.

At least, as quickly as you can with two small children clinging to you.

Back on the stairs, a noblewoman wearing a wide hoop skirt is walking in your direction. You think fast.

What now? Maybe if you bring the children to the kitchen, you'll get a chance to take Yitzchak away while the girl eats her eels.

But with every extra second you spend in the castle, you increase the chance that you or Yitzchak will be recognized — or that you'll run into the blue-eyed man.

To take both children to the kitchen, turn to page 103.

To hand the girl over to the noblewoman, turn to page 105.

"Actually," you say, "I was sent by the boy's nursemaid. She said I should bring him to her."

The woman squints at you suspiciously. "I'm told this boy is important. Nobody is supposed to take him, except by order of the king."

"Um ...," you say. "I think the king was the one who told her to tell me to ... uh ... I mean ..."

Her eyes narrow. She steps sideways, so that she is standing between you and Yitzchak.

"Never mind," you stammer. "I — I must have made a mistake. I'm looking for a different child."

You start to back away. But just then, Yitzchak shouts your name gleefully.

"Who did you say you are?" the woman says suspiciously.

You open your mouth, then close it. You don't know what to say.

"Get behind me, Johanna," the woman says to the girl. Without waiting to see if the girl obeys (she doesn't), the woman opens her mouth to shout.

But instead of a scream, what comes out of her mouth is a strangled "Aaackk!" She pitches forward and lands flat on her face.

Yitzchak untangles himself from her legs and continues running toward you.

The little girl laughs. The woman growls.

You grab Yitzchak, and then you turn and run, faster than you have ever run before.

You run so fast that it takes you only minutes to reach Don Abarbanel's house, and safety.

Turn to page 133.

THE LITTLE GIRL LEADS you to the castle kitchen. It is large and busy, filled with shouts and clangs and the smell of garlic and saffron. Overwhelmed, you stop in the doorway. But the little girl, again, knows exactly where to go. She pulls her hand out of yours and walks over to a woman who is busy stirring a large bowl of stew.

And there it is: your chance.

You turn on your heel and stride out of the kitchen, pulling Yitzchak behind you. The stairs are right there. All you have to do is get out without meeting anyone. Then it's straight downhill to the Jewish Quarter. If you run, you'll be at Don Abarbanel's home in only —

"NO!" Yitzchak screams.

He throws himself backward, making you stagger and stop. It

is all you can do to keep your grip on his hand.

"WANT EELS!" Yitzchak shouts, loudly enough to make several kitchen maids look your way. One of them grins at you in sympathy. The other sniffs and turns back to the dishes she is washing.

"Yitzchak!" you say. "Hush!"

"WANT EELS!" He flings himself sideways and pulls free of your grasp. You snatch at him and manage to snag his other arm a second before he escapes into the kitchen.

"EEEEEEEELS!"

To pick up Yitzchak and carry him out screaming, turn to page 110.

To try to calm him down, turn to page 108.

"I'M SORRY, MY LADY," you say. "Can you take this girl to the kitchen?"

The woman stops short. She adjusts her cap and pushes back the veil of fine cloth falling over her shoulders. Her eyes are wide with shock.

You forgot: Noblewomen do not take care of small children. Not even their own! Certainly not someone else's.

And you have made a grave mistake, because *this* noblewoman is not just shocked. She is suspicious. Her eyebrows draw together, and she frowns.

"I'm sorry!" you say. "I, er, I did not recognize you. Please forgive me."

She purses her lips. "Who are you, exactly?"

"I—uh—"

"Pardon me!" someone says, and you turn.

A pale-faced man wearing a low brown cap is tapping his foot impatiently behind you. "You are in my way," he says. "I need to see the queen."

"Don Santangel," the noblewoman greets him. Her voice is polite, but tinged with scorn. "The queen is currently in audience, with another ... Jew."

The man's face turns red.

Santangel. You recognize the name; you've heard it before. Luis de Santangel, like Don Abarbanel, is an important man at court. But though Don Santangel is a Jew by birth, he is officially a Christian. His grandfather converted to Christianity years ago, to save his life during riots against the Jews; now his children and grandchildren are trapped in the Christian faith, and have been raised without knowing much about their true religion. There are many Jews like that in Spain. Some of them practice Judaism in secret, but you've never heard that Don Santangel is one of them.

(Though maybe that just means he's very careful. The Inquisition is always on the lookout for secret Jews, so they must become good at hiding.)

"Very well," Don Santangel says stiffly. "I need to speak to Don Zacuto first, in any case."

"Don Zacuto? The rabbi astronomer, who made those new charts of the sky for sailors? Yes, I heard he was at court." Now the noblewoman looks intrigued. "Is it true that he is helping Don Christopher Columbus, and that you have convinced the queen to finance that mad voyage? I heard that Don Columbus has given up on Queen Isabella and is planning to go beg the king of France for money instead!" She leans forward, eager for gossip.

"Do not believe every rumor you hear," Don Santangel says. "I believe Queen Isabella may be changing her mind about Don Columbus's voyage. But she needs a loan from me to finance his ships, and I want to talk to Don Zacuto before I make up my mind."

The noblewoman shrugs. "If you want to throw your money into the sea, I suppose that's your business. But I have no idea where Don Zacuto is."

They both look at you.

You hesitate. If you say you can find Don Zacuto, you can get away from the suspicious woman. But you have no idea where Don Zacuto is! Once Don Santangel realizes that, will he help you? Or will he turn you in, to prove his own loyalty to the Christian faith?

To go with Don Santangel, turn to page 130.

To admit you don't know what he's talking about, turn to page 132.

"YITZCHAK!" YOU BEND DOWN and lower your voice. "You need to come with me. It's important."

"EELS!"

"You can't have eels!" you whisper. "They're not kosher!"

Yitzchak blinks at you, then pouts. But when he speaks, his voice is a bit lower. "Want candy!"

"Of course!" you say. "As much candy as you want. Just as soon as we get home."

Yitzchak sniffles, then nods.

Some of the kitchen maids are still watching you, but none of them call out or follow you.

You fly down the stairs. When you reach the bottom, you almost run into the woman from the courtyard. She steps back and frowns at you. "Where's Johanna?"

"In the kitchen," you say. "Throwing a screaming fit. You had better hurry!"

The woman rushes up the stairs, and you and Yitzchak run the other way.

You run so fast that it takes you only minutes to reach Don Abarbanel's house, and safety.

Turn to page 136.

YOU PICK UP YITZCHAK and march out of the kitchen. He screams and flails in your arms, and it is all you can do not to drop him — or to trip and fall yourself.

One of his little fists hits you in the eye. You shout in pain, and that startles him into silence — long enough for you to make it to the bottom of the stairs. But as you start down the hallway that will lead you out of the castle, he lets out a wail and screams, "Want go BACK!"

Unfortunately, it is at that moment that the woman from the courtyard turns into the hallway and comes face to face with you. She stops short.

"Where are you taking that child?" she demands.

"Um —"

"WANT EELS!" Yitzchak shrieks into your ear.

"I, uh —"

"WANT EELS NOW!"

The woman's eyes narrow. "Where is Johanna?"

"In the kitchen," you gasp. "She is fine. It's just that, um —" Yitzchak's wailing is making it hard to think. "He has a stomach-ache! I'm taking him to the doctor to get an infusion of ginger root."

"The doctor is that way." The woman points back the way you've come. "Down the hall, up the stairs, and to your right."

You have no choice but to turn and go back upstairs. Yitzchak switches over to shouting, "NO MEDICINE! DON'T WANT!"

As soon as you are out of the woman's earshot, you swing Yitzchak to the floor and kneel in front of him, holding him firmly by the shoulders.

"No medicine?" you say.

"NO MEDICINE!"

"Then we have to get out of here before someone tries to give you medicine," you say. "Can you help me do that?"

Yitzchak considers it. You hold your breath.

Then he nods.

"All right," you say. "So we have to sneak out *very quietly*."

Yitzchak looks at you suspiciously. He opens his mouth.

"Otherwise," you whisper, "the doctor will hear us, and come quickly with the medicine!"

Yitzchak's eyes widen. He nods solemnly.

Your mother will not be too happy with you the next time Yitzchak really is sick, and *she* has to give him medicine.

"Okay," you whisper. You hold out your hand and Yitzchak takes it. "Come with me."

"Come with you where?" a familiar voice asks, from right behind you.

This time, you're the one who screams. But you muffle your shriek right away as you recognize the voice. You straighten and turn.

The boy standing behind you is your friend, Shimon Seneor. His grandfather, like Don Abarbanel, has an important position in the castle. Shimon, who is being trained to take over the position someday, is in the castle often.

Your breath rushes out of you in relief. Quickly, you explain everything that's happened. Shimon's eyes widen.

"We need to go to my grandfather," he says when you're done. "He'll be able to explain everything."

"Are you sure?" you say. "Maybe we should just leave."

Shimon shakes his head. "The court is full of rivalries and intrigue. If the wrong person sees us, it could cause all sorts of trouble for my grandfather and Don Abarbanel. They need to know what's going on."

"All right," you say gratefully. "Let's go, quickly."

Turn to page 113.

SHIMON LEADS YOU THROUGH the castle, walking so fast he is almost running. Before long, Yitzchak gets tired, and you pick him up and carry him.

Finally, you reach a room with a slightly open door.

"Shimon?" You recognize the voice: It is Don Avraham Seneor, Shimon's grandfather and Don Abarbanel's friend. "Come in, quickly, and close the door."

Shimon walks into the room without hesitation. But you hang back for a moment, holding Yitzchak tight.

Maybe your first instinct was right. Maybe you *should* leave.

To follow him, turn to page 117.

To leave, turn to page 114.

"I'm sorry," you say, backing away.

"Wait." Shimon turns back. "What are you doing? You have to —"

"I have to go." You turn, meaning to walk away with dignity. But there is a prickle between your shoulder blades, and the next thing you know, you find yourself running.

Your feet slap loudly on the carpet as you run with all your might, Yitzchak held tightly in your arms. Shimon shouts your name, but you don't stop.

You turn left, and then right, trying to remember the way you came. But instead of the stairs, you find yourself at a window. Below you, the city of Toledo sprawls gray among the green hills, the river curving in a dark gleam beneath it.

You turn and run the other way, and this time you almost

collide with a noblewoman who is stepping out of her bedroom. She draws back and gasps.

"I'm sorry!" you pant, and turn again, racing down the hall — and then, somehow, you are back at the top of the stairs. You hurtle down them so fast that Yitzchak screams.

When you are finally out of the castle, you risk a glance back. No one is following you.

You focus on the path ahead, on flying down the slope without dropping Yitzchak or falling. You don't stop running until you are in the Jewish Quarter. And even then, you walk as quickly as you can.

Your heart does not stop pounding until you are in Don Abarbanel's home.

Turn to page 142.

YOU FOLLOW CLOSE BEHIND Shimon and shut the door behind you. As soon as you loosen your grip on him, Yitzchak pulls away. You let go of him, and he goes to examine a standing mirror in the corner of the room.

Shimon's grandfather, Don Seneor, glances at him before focusing on Shimon. "I'm glad you're here. There is something I must tell you." He looks at you. "And you should hear it, too."

"What is going on?" you say.

"Sit down." Don Seneor gestures to a carved wooden chair.

Reluctantly, you sit. Don Seneor clasps his hands behind his back.

"Don Abarbanel and I have failed," he says sadly. "Despite all our entreaties, and all our bribes, we cannot change the king's mind. He is going to expel all the Jews from Spain."

You cover your mouth with your hands.

"We will have three months to leave. And we will not be allowed to take anything we own with us." Don Seneor paces across the room. His satin shoes make almost no sound on the thick carpet. "There are very few places where we can go. Most people, probably, will cross the border to Portugal. But Don Abarbanel cannot even do that. He has too many enemies in the Portuguese court." He lifts one eyebrow. "Including, unfortunately, the king of Portugal."

Why is he telling you this?

"A journey by ship will cost a fortune. And pirates will be waiting, as soon as they hear what is happening here." Don Seneor turns to face you. "But there is one other option."

Turn to page 119.

YOU STARE AT DON Seneor, waiting for him to go on. But he looks at his grandson.

Shimon looks down, and you realize that he knows what his grandfather is going to say. Their family must have already discussed this.

"Convert to Christianity," Shimon fills in, without meeting your eyes. "If we become Christians, we can stay, and we can keep everything."

You find your voice. "You can't mean it!"

"It is an impossible choice," Don Seneor says sadly. "But one that every single one of us is going to have to make. And we have made ours."

You stare at him, then whirl around to look at Shimon. This time, your friend does meet your gaze.

"I'm sorry," Shimon says. "But my family is staying here. As Christians."

You are too shocked to say anything.

"We have no choice," Shimon says, in a pleading voice. "Our family has lived here for generations. This is our home. We can't leave."

Your family has been Jewish for longer than you have been Spanish, you think. But you don't say it, because you understand Shimon. Who could possibly bear to leave Spain behind forever?

"You can stay, too," Shimon adds.

"No!" you say.

"Your conversion doesn't have to be real. Secretly, in your heart—and when you're alone in your home—you can still be a Jew. But you will keep your home and your family. If you and your mother leave—where will you go? Who will take you in?"

You don't know the answer to that, and Shimon sees it in your face. He leans forward.

"Just think about it," he says. "Promise me you'll consider it."

Your fists clench. You want to tell him no. That you will always be a faithful Jew, no matter what.

But he is your friend. You don't want to lose him. You don't want to lose everything you have and everything you know.

To say no, turn to page 121.

To say you'll think about it, turn to page 125.

To grab Yitzchak and run, turn to page 129.

"NO!" YOU SAY. "I am a Jew, and I will be a Jew forever."

Don Seneor draws himself up. But there is no anger in his eyes. There is only pain.

You have seen that agonized look on his face before. You've passed by, more than once, as he and Don Abarbanel sat together, working on one of their projects. Raising money to ransom Jewish captives, or working to protect converted Jews from the Inquisition, or just learning together.

How can someone like Don Seneor even think about such a betrayal?

But he's so old now; would he even survive the long, arduous journey from Spain?

Spain is full of Jews who have converted to Christianity. It's almost normal by now.

Almost.

You look at Shimon, instead of at Don Seneor, when you speak. "You will be a Jew forever, too. You'll always know the truth about yourself. And about what you did."

Shimon looks down at the carpet. Don Seneor draws in a deep breath, but says nothing.

Neither of them tries to stop you when you turn and run.

You find Don Abarbanel in his study, with a quill in his hand. Despite all his important duties at the castle, Don Abarbanel's true love is learning and writing. He has already written lengthy commentaries on the Torah.

After a second glance, though, you can see that Don Abarbanel is not writing a Torah commentary right now. His face is troubled, and he is holding the quill tightly without dipping it into the ink.

He turns and sees you, and his face softens. "What's the matter? Is it important? I just returned from talking to Queen Isabella, and it did not go well. It is ... a very tense time. I need to think."

"I'm sorry," you whisper. "But it is important."

He frowns. "What happened?"

You take a deep breath and tell him everything. As you speak, your tears begin to fall, and you don't try to stop them.

Don Abarbanel puts the quill down, his back straightening. His face grows pale.

"I'm sorry," you finish. By now, you are sobbing so hard you

can barely get the words out. "I left Yitzchak there. I didn't know what else to do."

"At least you did the right thing by coming to me." He rushes past you out the door. "Stay here!" he calls over his shoulder. "Wait for me."

Turn to page 98.

"I understand what you're telling me," you say. "I will think about it."

The words taste like dust in your mouth. But Shimon smiles happily, and you cannot help but smile back.

"You'll be glad," he says. "Especially if the Abarbanel family also stays."

"Don Abarbanel will never convert to Christianity," you say.

It's true that over the past hundred years, many Spanish Jews have given in to the constant persecution and declared themselves to be Christians. But you think of Don Abarbanel sitting in his study, night after night, writing his commentary on the Torah, and you are sure. "There is nothing that would make him abandon his faith."

Shimon's gaze darts to the corner, where Yitzchak is making

faces at himself in the gold-framed mirror.

Your blood runs cold. Slowly, you say, "I think you're right. I must convince my mother, though."

"You don't need your mother's permission," Don Seneor says. "And you must not tell her anything that happened here."

"I won't," you say.

You can't tell if Don Seneor believes you. But when Shimon leads you out of the room, his grandfather does not protest.

The two of you walk through the courtyard and down the hill. Yitzchak is so tired that you have to carry him, and you are soon out of breath. You are glad, because it gives you an excuse not to talk.

You can't think of a single thing to say.

By the time you reach Don Abarbanel's house, Yitzchak has fallen asleep in your arms. Shimon bids you farewell as you head to your mother's room.

Your mother is sewing lace onto a collar. She looks up and smiles when she sees you. Then she takes a closer look at your face, and her smile disappears.

"What's wrong?" she says.

You lay Yitzchak down carefully on the bed. He turns over on his side, and his chest rises and falls peacefully. His eyelids are tightly shut.

"Come with me, Mother," you say. "Please. There is something I must tell Don Abarbanel. And you should hear it, too."

Continue to page 127.

DON ABARBANEL'S STUDY IS a small, elegant room, full of Hebrew books and the smell of ink. As he listens to you, Don Abarbanel pushes his inkwell aside. He closes his eyes briefly and rubs his forehead.

"I am so sorry," you say when you are done. Your voice trembles. Your mother takes your hand and holds it tightly.

"Do not be sorry," Don Abarbanel says. "I owe you my thanks for uncovering this terrible plot. The rulers thought they could baptize my grandson and thus force me to convert to Christianity." He shakes his head, then looks at your mother. "We must send Yitzchak out of Spain immediately. I will have a carriage prepared. Will you take him to my sister in Portugal?"

"Of course," your mother says.

"Thank you." Don Abarbanel looks around his study, and his

shoulders droop. Then he straightens. "It will take more time to prepare the rest of the household to leave. But at least I will know that Yitzchak — and you — are safe. I will make arrangements, and we will rejoin each other in one of the Italian states. We will make a new life there."

Turn to page 141.

YOUR HEART THUDS AGAINST your ribs as you run with all your might. You hold Yitzchak tightly in your arms, and for once, he doesn't fight you. Shimon shouts your name, but you don't slow down.

You gasp in air that hurts your throat, waiting—for a yell, the sound of footsteps, maybe even an arrow whistling toward your back. But nothing happens, and you manage to get out of the castle without being stopped. As you fly down the steep slope, toward the city sprawling along the hills below, you risk a glance back.

No one is following you.

You don't stop running until you are in the Jewish Quarter. And even then, you walk as quickly as you can.

Your heart does not stop pounding until you are inside Don Abarbanel's home.

Turn to page 133.

"I KNOW WHERE DON ZACUTO is," you say quickly. "I can take you to him. But, er, this girl is hungry —"

"Very well," the noblewoman says irritably. "I will find someone to take charge of her. What about the boy?"

You tighten your fingers around Yitzchak's small hand.

"I know where he needs to go," you say. "It is on our way."

A moment of silence. Don Santangel humphs impatiently.

"Follow me," you say, and pull Yitzchak past the noblewoman.

To your relief, nobody protests. When you look back, Don Santangel is right behind you, but the noblewoman and the little girl are nowhere to be seen.

"You don't need to lead me through the palace," Don Santangel says. He doesn't sound angry; he sounds amused. "I'm the king's finance minister. I know my way around. Just tell me where Don Zacuto is."

You swallow hard. "I … I don't know where he is. I'm sorry."

Don Santangel looks at you. You back away from him, dragging Yitzchak with you.

"Don't worry," Don Santangel says. "I will find him myself." He glances into the castle, then looks back at you. His eyes are sharp, not with anger, but with something closer to sadness. "For now, I think you had better leave the castle, and take that boy with you."

"Thank you," you whisper.

And you lose no time in following his advice.

Turn to page 133.

"I'M SORRY," YOU SAY. "I ... I don't know where he is. I would try to help you, but ... um ..."

"But we're hungry!" the girl shouts, and pulls her hand out of yours. "I want to eat *right now*!"

"Right now!" Yitzchak echoes gleefully.

The girl races past the noblewoman, dodging around her hoop skirt. You have no choice but to follow, muttering a quick apology as you drag Yitzchak behind you. You finally reach the girl and grab her hand, and only then do you dare look behind you. The noblewoman, and Don Santangel, are nowhere to be seen.

You breathe a quick sigh of relief.

"Kitchen!" the girl says, and stamps her foot.

"All right," you say. "Let's go get you something to eat."

Turn to page 103.

MUCH LATER, AFTER EVERYTHING has been explained and Yitzchak is sound asleep, Don Abarbanel summons you to his study.

"I am very grateful to you," he says. "Thanks to your quick thinking, and with Hashem's help, we were able to save Yitzchak from a terrible plot."

You almost smile. But there is something in Don Abarbanel's tone that makes you look down and wait, instead.

"But I was not successful in saving the rest of us." Don Abarbanel shakes his head. "Nothing — not reason or money or morality — will change the monarchs' minds. In just three months, every Jew in Spain must convert to Christianity, or leave forever."

You look up. Don Abarbanel's face is drawn and sad, but his gaze is direct.

"Where will you go?" you whisper.

"I believe my best option is to travel to the Italian states. There are many rulers there who will be interested in hiring me to help with their finances." Don Abarbanel leans forward. "Your mother, of course, will come with us. As will you, if you want to."

If you *want* to? What does that mean? What other choice do you have?

"You met one of Don Columbus's friends today and he was very impressed with your quick thinking," Don Abarbanel says. "He tells me he can get you onto one of Columbus's ships."

You stare, speechless.

"You would, of course, have to hide who you are. But then, so will many of us." Don Abarbanel sighs. "You need to understand. It is very risky. The disguise would be difficult to maintain. And even if you get away with it, most people believe the world is too large for Columbus's ships to make it all the way around. Chances are his ships will sink, or run out of food, before he ever gets to the Indies. But if Columbus is right ... well, then you may find yourself with opportunities you never even dreamed of."

You still can't think of anything to say.

"It's a serious decision," Don Abarbanel says. "Talk to your mother. Think about it for a few days. Whatever you choose, your life will never be the same." He blinks, and his eyes are bright with tears. "Though the same is now true for every Jew in Spain."

Sleep on it (or pretend you did), and then …

To go with Don Abarbanel, turn to page 153.

To sail with Columbus, turn to page 155.

YOU TELL YOUR MOTHER everything that has happened, and she immediately goes to Don Abarbanel. When she returns, she looks concerned, but not frightened.

"There are terrible plots being hatched in the castle," she says. "But Don Abarbanel is aware of them now. He knows what to do. He said to thank you."

She smiles, a bit shakily. "And *I* say it is time for you to go to bed."

Turn to page 141.

"AAAUUUGGHHHH!"

Even you didn't know you could scream that loud.

"WAAAAHHHHH!"

But Yitzchak is still louder.

Both of your screams, together, must be loud enough to reach the castle.

The man dumps Yitzchak back on the bed. Yitzchak flails and kicks the blanket, and one of his feet hits your mother in the face. Her eyes pop open, and now all three of you are screaming.

Outside the room, a door slams, and footsteps come running.

The man turns back to the window. In the bright moonlight, you see his face. It is the blue-eyed man who approached you on the road!

Your bed is closest to the window. If you lunge, maybe you can grab his ankles and pull him down.

Or you can get kicked in the face.

And even if you succeed — what then? What if no one else gets here in time? What if he has a knife?

He's *leaving*. Maybe you should just let him leave.

As you crouch on your bed, he hoists himself up to the window.

It's now or never. What are you going to do?

To grab his ankles, turn to page 73.

To let him go, turn to page 79.

"I UNDERSTAND WHAT YOU'RE TELLING me," you say. "I will think about it."

The words taste like dust in your mouth. But Shimon smiles widely.

"You'll be glad," he says. "Especially if the Abarbanel family also stays."

"Don Abarbanel will never convert to Christianity," you say.

It's true that over the past hundred years, many Spanish Jews have given in to the constant persecution and declared themselves to be Christians. But you think of Don Abarbanel sitting in his study, night after night, writing his commentary on the Torah, and you are sure. "There is nothing that would make him abandon the Torah."

"Perhaps you are right," Don Seneor says. Unlike Shimon, he

is not smiling. "Don Abarbanel is stronger than I am. But are *you* that strong?"

You blink back tears. "I … I have to talk to my mother."

"You don't need your mother's permission to convert," Don Seneor says. "And you must not tell her anything that happened here."

"I won't," you say.

You can't tell if Don Seneor believes you. But when you let yourself out, he does not protest.

And Shimon does not follow you. You wish he would, but you are also glad he does not.

When you reach Don Abarbanel's home, you go straight to your mother's room. Your mother is busy sewing lace onto a collar, but she looks up and smiles when she sees you. Then she takes a closer look at your face, and her smile disappears.

"What's wrong?" she says.

"Come with me, Mother," you say. "Please. There is something I must tell Don Abarbanel. And you should hear it, too."

Turn to page 127.

YOU DON'T KNOW WHAT tomorrow will bring. But that night, you snuggle under your blanket, listening to your mother's deep breathing and Yitzchak's snuffling snores. No matter what happens next, you will be with the people you love, and you know that Hashem will keep you safe.

Your lips curl into a smile as you bury your face in your pillow and fall deeply asleep.

— *The End* —

Want to see what else might have happened? Turn back to the beginning and find out where different choices might have led you ….

Don Abarbanel's home is not as grand as the castle, of course, but it is large and well-decorated, the entrance hall warmed by a large metal brazier filled with lighted coals. You bolt up the staircase and head straight for the room you share with your mother.

Your mother meets you at the door. "Where have you been? Yitzchak must be hungry!"

You open your mouth, then close it. You're not sure what to tell her. And before you can think of where to begin, she snatches Yitzchak away and bustles him into the house.

After that, things are so busy that you don't get a chance to speak. By the time she is tucking you into bed, you are too tired to say anything.

You're safe, after all. Yitzchak is safe. For now, that is enough.

Will you ever find out what the blue-eyed man really wanted? Not in this lifetime ...

— The End —

....

Want to get closer to the truth? Turn back to the beginning and find out where different choices might have led you ....

"INDEED I DID." DON Abarbanel leans down so that his face is directly across from yours. "Thank you. Because of your courage and quick thinking, and with Hashem's help, we have escaped a terrible plot. I owe my grandson's safety to you."

You say something that comes out sounding like, "*Gah — ah — blark.*"

Don Abarbanel's eyes are deep and wise. "There will be difficult times ahead for the Jewish people. But as long as we remain faithful to Hashem, we will make it through. Just like the *malach* of Eisav could hurt Yaakov but not kill him, the Spanish monarchs may cause us terrible suffering, but they can never destroy us completely. Do you understand?"

You nod.

Don Abarbanel straightens. "You and your mother will always

have a place with my family. I will make sure you are both safe."

This time, you manage actual words. "Thank you."

Don Abarbanel smiles and turns to leave.

Even before the door closes behind him, Yitzchak throws himself at you, grabbing you around the legs. He knocks you off balance, and you both fall to the floor. Instead of scolding him, you wrap your arms around him and hug him tightly. You sit there, holding each other and laughing, until your mother comes to call you to bed.

— The End —

Want to see what else might have happened? Turn back to the beginning and find out where different choices might have led you ....

By the time you get to Don Abarbanel's home, the news has already spread. People stream toward the synagogue to give thanks to Hashem. In the street, everyone is laughing and talking. It's like a heavy cloud has been lifted from the Jewish Quarter.

Some time later, when Don Abarbanel comes from the castle, he has Yitzchak by his side. You run to Yitzchak, twirl him around, and hold him tight.

Don Abarbanel smiles as he watches you.

Together, the three of you walk into the synagogue, while all around you, the Jews of the city rejoice.

— The End —

Want to see what else might have happened? Turn back to the beginning and find out where different choices might have led you ....

THE HOURS DRAG ON, and Don Abarbanel does not return. But your mother comes to find you.

When you tell her what has happened, you burst into tears again. This time, you are not alone. You and your mother are sitting in Don Abarbanel's study, leaning on each other while your tears dry, when Don Abarbanel finally returns.

He has Yitzchak with him.

You start crying all over again as you hold out your arms. Yitzchak runs into them, and you hold him tight. He looks perfectly fine. He is not hurt.

But Don Abarbanel's face is grave.

"We must all get ready to go," he says. "Immediately."

"Why?" your mother says. "Was it a misunderstanding?"

"Unfortunately, no." Don Abarbanel lets out a breath. "Don Seneor and I have failed to save the Jews of Spain. The king is issuing the order of expulsion, despite all we have done."

Your mother gasps and presses her hands to her mouth.

"But the king wants me to stay," Don Abarbanel goes on. "He asked me to convert to Christianity. I said no, of course. And so, it seems, a plot was hatched to kidnap my grandson and baptize him. Then I would have faced a choice between converting, or losing Yitzchak forever."

"But the plot was foiled?" you say hopefully.

Don Abarbanel looks at you sadly. "No. Yitzchak was baptized. I was able to get there in time to take him back, but according to law, he is no longer ours. So we must steal him away, immediately, to someplace where Christian laws do not apply. We must go to the Ottoman Empire."

"No!" your mother gasps. The Ottoman Empire is far away, a perilous journey by ship.

"We must go tonight," Don Abarbanel goes on. "We must leave everything behind." He looks into his study, at his books and papers, and shakes his head sadly. "I will not force you to come with me. But understand that in three months, we will all have to leave, no matter what."

"Of course we will come with you," your mother says.

You press your face into Yitzchak's cheek.

You may be leaving everything you own behind. But the most important things will still be with you.

— The End —

Want to see what else might have happened? Turn back to the beginning and find out where different choices might have led you ....

DON ABARBANEL WORKS DAY and night to get Yitzchak back. But nobody can tell you how much progress he's made.

The decree is announced from the castle a few days later. "All Jews have three months in which to convert to Christianity, or leave the Spanish Peninsula forever. You may not take any gold, silver, or precious stones with you."

Your mother says the two of you might as well leave at once, before the mass exodus begins. After all, you have nothing to take with you, anyhow. And she has no job anymore.

Your mother weeps every night for Yitzchak. She feels guilty — but also, she loves him, and she misses him.

You miss him, too. Every night, you stare at the castle and wish he was back here, where he belongs. Every day, you pray that he will be saved.

So you make no argument as you and your mother gather together your meager belongings. Don Abarbanel gives your mother a parting gift—enough money to last you for several months, until you can, maybe, find a new way to make money. His kindness makes you want to cry.

On the morning of your departure, you wake up to hear a familiar laugh. You jump out of bed and race down the stairs.

Don Abarbanel is sitting in the entrance hall, and on his lap is Yitzchak!

You race over, grab Yitzchak, and hug him. The fruit pie he is eating leaves sticky smears all over your face, but you don't even care.

"How did you do it?" You are too happy, for the moment, to be shy. "How did you get him back?"

"With Hashem's help," Don Abarbanel says simply. "You don't need to worry about the details." He rubs one hand over his eyes. "But we must send Yitzchak to safety at once. I will need your mother to take him to my sister, in Portugal."

And so, that very day, you and your mother set off on the long, dusty road, with the sun beating down on your heads. You aren't the only ones leaving early; tens of thousands of Jews will have to leave, and dozens of them are trudging down the road with you.

Don Abarbanel isn't leaving—not quite yet. He hopes to arrange for another position, at another court, where he can help some of the refugees.

"Once we are settled," you hear him telling his wife, "we will bring Yitzchak to join us. With Hashem's help, we will all be together again."

As you walk, you pray extra hard. Not just for Yitzchak and for Don Abarbanel, but for you and your mother, and for all the Jews of Spain.

Together, you start on the long, dangerous journey toward the border of Portugal, leaving the city of Toledo and the country of Spain behind you forever.

— The End —

Want to see what else might have happened? Turn back to the beginning and find out where different choices might have led you ....

THE SHIP IS OVERCROWDED, the captain is mean, and the sailors treat all the Jews with contempt. But Don Abarbanel is calm and certain, helping to make sure everyone is safe and leading the Jews in prayer as the ship launches into the vast blue sea. Once everyone is settled, he comes to stand beside you at the rail. Together, you watch the shoreline of Spain recede farther and farther away.

You clear your throat. "Where … where are we going, in the end?"

"Naples, in the south of Italy. The king of Naples is in need of my services." The ocean rushes away from you in long, flat waves. "With Hashem's help, I hope to gain an important position at his court, and use it to help make Naples a new home for the Jewish refugees from Spain."

You swallow hard. "What if we are thrown out of Naples, too?"

"It could happen. I do not put my trust in kings. It is always dangerous for one man to have that much power." Don Abarbanel turns, one hand on the rail. "Whether we remain in Naples, or are forced to leave, will depend upon Hashem's plan."

Normally, you would not dare speak up at a moment like this. But there is something in Don Abarbanel's eyes. As if he is waiting for you to ask.

"And what is happening to us now?" you burst out. You turn back to the shore. You can no longer see the thousands of penniless refugees who are still there, waiting desperately for a ship to carry them away from the land they love. "Is this part of Hashem's plan?"

"Yes." Don Abarbanel meets your gaze directly. His eyes are clear. "Hashem promised Avraham that we will be like the stars. Just like the stars sometimes cast bright light and sometimes are hidden by darkness, the Jewish nation will have periods when we descend into sadness. But just like the stars are under the control of Hashem, so are we. We exist under His protection, and we will emerge from even this tragedy."

The dark blue waves grow vaster, until you can no longer see Spain at all. You turn and look instead at the waters ahead of you, shattering into ripples of white froth as the ship plunges through them, carrying you to a new home.

— The End —

Want to see what else might have happened? Turn back to the beginning and find out where different choices might have led you ....

It is a glorious day. The blue, glassy waves crash in slow motion against the shore. The calm of the sea is in contrast to the chaos and confusion on land, where Jews crowd the port, desperate to get onto a ship.

But you are pretending that has nothing to do with you. You have to.

"What a fleet of misery and woe," Columbus says, from behind you. You almost jump out of your skin, but you manage a nod, and after a moment, he passes by.

You are dressed in the clothes of a Christian boy, you have given your name as Hernando, and you are doing your best to avoid the rough sailors. You miss your mother. You are terrified.

And you are beginning to suspect that you might be getting seasick.

But despite all that, there is a flutter of excitement in your stomach. Columbus and his sailors are sure they are going to find a new route to the Indies. Here, surrounded by their certainty, other people's doubts don't seem to matter.

This voyage could change everything. Not just for you, but for the whole world! And whatever happens, you will be part of it.

The sails billow in the wind, the ship plunges through the waves, and you hold tight to the slick wooden rail, wondering what surprises the wide blue ocean has in store.

— The End —

Want to see what else might have happened? Turn back to the beginning and find out where different choices might have led you ....

When you are finished talking, Don Abarbanel sits completely still. Then he says, "Thank you. This is valuable information. Now I can see to it that Yitzchak is safe. I owe that to you."

You hesitate. Then you blurt, "I broke a promise."

"What do you mean?"

"The man who … who tried to take Yitzchak. I promised him that if he told me the truth, I would let him out. And then I didn't. I *lied.*" Your eyes sting. You open them wide to keep the tears back. You don't want to cry in front of Don Abarbanel.

Don Abarbanel steps out from behind his desk. To your astonishment, he kneels on the floor right next to you, so he can look you in the eye.

"You are a child," he says. "No adult should ever ask you to do something your mother wouldn't want you to do. And if anyone asks you to promise something you know is wrong, you are allowed to ignore him."

You nod. Don Abarbanel puts his hand on your shoulder.

"My grandson will be safe because of you," he says. "Thank you." He rises to his feet and leads you out of the study. "There will be difficult times ahead for the Jewish people. But as long as we are all together, and remain faithful to Hashem, we will make it through. You and your mother will always have a place with my family. I will make sure you are both cared for. And I can tell you this: You made the right choice."

Now, you *are* crying. But you don't mind.

"Thank you," you say.

And as you head back to your mother's room, you find yourself, confusingly, smiling and crying at the same time.

— The End —

Want to see what else might have happened? Turn back to the beginning and find out where different choices might have led you ....

Epilogue

There really was a plot to kidnap the grandson of Don Yitzchak Abarbanel.

In 1492, King Ferdinand of Aragon and Queen Isabella of Castile signed an order expelling all Jews from the Spanish Peninsula. This came as a complete shock to the Jews, who had lived in Spain for centuries. In fact, three of the rulers' financial advisors — Don Seneor, Don Melamed, and Don Abarbanel — were Jewish. They were greatly valued by the king and queen, and used their influence to protect their fellow Jews.

But even those three men could not change the king's mind. They begged him, they reasoned with him, and they offered an enormous bribe. Don Abarbanel gained an audience with the queen and made a daring, dangerous speech (which you may have heard, if your choices led you to eavesdrop).

But the rulers would not budge. The Jews were given a choice: convert, or leave.

The rulers' Jewish advisors were strongly pressured to convert. If they did, the king and queen would not lose the benefit of their advice. Meanwhile, their conversion would weaken the resolve of the rest of the Jews. Don Seneor and Don Melamed gave in to the royal pressure. But Don Abarbanel refused. Nothing, it soon became clear, would convince him to abandon Judaism.

So a plot was devised to kidnap his one-year-old grandson and convert the child to Christianity. Then his parents, if they wanted to keep him, would have to convert as well. And if they did, Don Abarbanel would face the choice of either converting or losing his entire family.

In real life, the Abarbanels learned of the plan in time — though we don't know how. They swiftly sent the child away with his nurse. The nurse fled across the nearest border to Portugal, where she and Yitzchak probably lived with Don Abarbanel's sister. Don Abarbanel, meanwhile, fled to Italy. We have evidence that, after many hard years and many more plots, Yitzchak was reunited with his family.

This book contains some endings that are worse than what truly happened, and some that are better. I could not resist including one ending that is much, much happier than the one history gave us: an ending in which Don Abarbanel's attempts to stop the Spanish Expulsion were successful, and the Jews were never forced to leave.

In reality, events took place over a greater stretch of time —

and a greater variety of places — than in this story. Don Abarbanel lived in a town called Segura, near the border between Spain and Portugal, and Don Seneor lived in a different town. The decree of expulsion was actually signed in Granada, where the king and queen had established their frequently-moving court. But it was proclaimed several months later in the city of Toledo — which is where I chose to set this story.

It was also around this time that Christopher Columbus — called Cristobal Colon in Spanish — was planning his expedition to sail around the world. Queen Isabella signed off on his voyage three weeks after proclaiming the edict of expulsion, and he left on the same day as many of the conversos. Young boys were often sent to sea between the ages of eight and ten; girls disguised as boys, though there are a few known cases, were far less common. However, it is very likely that there were Jews on Columbus's ship.

Don Yitzchak Abarbanel lived the rest of his life in various Italian states, starting in the kingdom of Naples. Wherever he lived, he continued to serve as financial advisor to kings and rulers. But once out of Spain, his main focus was on writing and publishing. It was after the expulsion that he finished his masterful commentaries on the Torah, for which he is most well known today. The thoughts he shares in this book about exile, kings, and Jewish destiny are taken from his commentaries on Genesis, Deuteronomy, and the Book of Samuel.

But these are just snatches from his extensive, brilliant, and sometimes surprising commentaries — which one day, perhaps, you will read for yourself.

Acknowledgments

To all the kids, and kids at heart, who helped me test-drive this book:

My first readers: Shoshana Cypess, Hadassah Cypess, Dovid Cypess, Bella Kotek, Rachelli Mizrachi, Talya Cohen, Shlomo Sheril, Rochel Leah Suslovich, Baruch Kranz, and Avi Kranz.

My army of path-checkers: Micah Amster, Eliana Cohen, Harry Davidoff, Aryeh de Metz, Leah de Metz, Akiva Gordon, Tzipora Gordon, Devora Gorfajn, Eliezer Gorfajn, Aviva Haber, Adeline Huffmanparent, Sebastien Huffmanparent, Azaria Hileman, Shani Meyers, Nechunya Meyerowitz, Avigdor Pesach Peromsik, Tehilla Temima Peromsik, Levi Polyakov, Nate Schwarzmer, Malka Shnaidman, Yael Siesser, Tova Suslovich, Elisha Wittlin, Sarah Wunder, and Shoshana Wunder.

And to Aviva Werner, who listened to me babble about my idea for this book and said, "You have to write it!" Thank you for everything.